# WHY AM I NOT ENOUGH?

VENUKA GOYAL

Copyright © Venuka Goyal
All Rights Reserved.

# Contents

# Acknowledgements

I owe thanks to my sister Sharika and my good friend Namrata for their feedback on the initial drafts of this story.

# 1

In the eight years of their marriage, the last year or so had been the worst. It had been almost unbearable. Abhi couldn't remember the last time he had a conversation with Seema without getting into a fight or without at least one of them getting really rude. It was as if she hated him.

"How would you understand?" she would rant at him, "It's me who is going through all this! Why did I ever expect anything from you?"

There was rage. There was resentment. Where were the smiles? Where had all the fun gone? Where was the woman he had fallen in love with?

Abhi met Seema about eleven years ago at a friend's party.

"She's Teena's friend," his friend Atul had told him when he caught Abhi looking her way, "she's single."

Seema looked irresistible in her knee-length dress, the dark blue fabric complimenting her wheatish complexion. Her straight shoulder length hair framed her face just right and her luscious lips glittered invitingly as her eyes twinkled when she smiled. Atul offered to introduce him to her but Abhi decided to take matters into his own hands. He noticed that the glass in her hand was empty and as soon as the person she was talking to seemed distracted, he approached her with one drink in each hand.

"Hi I'm Abhimanyu. Atul's friend."

"Seema. Teena's friend."

"Would you like another drink?"

"Why not!"

By the time they parted ways that night, Abhi and Seema had exchanged phone numbers and Abhi couldn't wait to send a message to her when he reached his flat.

'You were right,' he joked, 'I'm not normal. I have 34 teeth,'

'How disappointing,' she responded, 'If you had 36 teeth I would have asked you out for dinner tomorrow night.'

'34 teeth deserve coffee at least'

'Maybe'

'6 PM, Brista?'

'Maybe'

'Good night'

'Sweet dreams'

He had, indeed, dreamt of her that night and when she showed up at the coffee shop at 6:10 PM the next evening, he was sure he was in big trouble. She looked so sexy in her flared black pants and sleeveless crop top.

"Sorry, the meeting ran late," she apologised as she took the seat in front of him.

"I don't think I've ever had my date apologised to me for being only 10 minutes late"

"I guess that means you're usually on time for dates. I like that in a man."

She was so confident and radiant and they had so much in common.

"Definitely Sci-fi over horror. Any day!" She agreed with him.

"Inception?" he asked her.

"Sure!"

"It's a date then."

Things were different at this juncture in their life though. Eight years into their marriage, they were living more like roommates who didn't really get along with each other. It had been over a year since they had watched a movie together. And whenever he suggested that they go for a trip abroad she would snap at him, "How can you even think about all that right now?"

It was like they were robots doing their jobs and getting home to eat the food that the cook had prepared for them and then going back to the office the next morning. The weekends were reserved for staying out of each other's hair so as not to start a fight. Abhi had taken to spending more time on his workouts at the gym and Seema had taken to reading books. Books that Abhi couldn't relate to. Books about people who never had kids out of choice and people who never had kids because of medical reasons and people who never had kids after their kids were no more. She also read books about people who had kids after prolonged medical treatment.

"The doctors tell you what to do and what to expect," Abhi would say to Seema, "Why do you want your whole life to revolve around it? Why can't you think about anything else?"

"How can you be so insensitive?" she would retaliate, "I thought you loved me. But you don't get me at all!"

There was a time when they used to get each other. There was a time they would be on the same page.

"How about Goa in December?" he had asked her the year before they got married.

"Sounds amazing! I'll book the resort," she replied.

"I'll book the flights," he volunteered.

They used to love travelling together and watching movies together and just being with each other. But not any more. In her obsession to have a baby, Seema had forgotten how to live.

The cream walls of the L-shaped waiting room made it look more roomy than it actually was. The walls were lined with grey metal chairs and on one end of the room was the door to the doctor's office. Seema was sitting on the chair right next to the door. And even though there were a handful of other people sitting in the room, Seema was all alone. Abhi couldn't be there with her that day. He had an important meeting that he couldn't get out of or so he had said that morning. Seema was no longer sure about anything he said to her. She always questioned the intention behind his every action. Why couldn't she trust him anymore? Seema had no clue. When the fertility clinic had asked for signatures of both husband and wife before getting the procedure started, she had half-expected Abhi to refuse to sign. She had spent a week imagining what she would do in such a scenario. How important was it for her to have a baby after all? Would she even be willing to divorce Abhi if he refused to let her do this? Maybe. Maybe not. She did love him still after all. But did she? These days her mind was so clouded with thoughts other than those of Abhi that she no longer remembered what being in love felt like. She had only one mission in her life right now. She wanted to have a baby. So that morning when Abhi had insisted that she get the doctor's appointment postponed by a day she had snapped back at him, "I'll go on my own. Anyway I usually go on my own when I get the injections."

"But..."

"I don't want to fight about this right now. I'm getting late for the office. I'll go there on my way back home."

She had tried to be brave but right now she was regretting this. Maybe she should have insisted he came along. Or maybe she should have agreed with him and postponed her appointment so that it was on a day when he could be there with her. Even though they had been fighting with each other a lot lately, it would still have been nice to have someone with her. But she couldn't do anything about it now. She was sitting there, waiting for the doctor to arrive, and her name was the first one on the register that was kept on the desk in front of her where the attendant sat guarding it. She would be the first one to get to see the doctor as soon as the doctor got there.

Most of the people in the waiting room were women. Some of them had their husband or a family member accompany them. Some of them didn't. The first time Seema had come to the fertility clinic she had noticed the age mentioned for many of the patients that were registered. It was weird. In the register where they jotted down their name when they came to the clinic, they had to write their age and their weight every time. For everyone to see. But it was fine. Seema was so desperate to have a baby that she didn't care about all the embarrassment and all the pain. She didn't care when the nurse treated her like an errant teenager when she checked her weight on the weighing scale every time. She didn't care when the pain from the repeated injections made her eyes well up with tears. She didn't care that the medication made her feel not quite herself. She didn't care when the doctor brought over interns to peer between her legs and learn how the procedure was done as she lay on the bed trying not to think about anything in particular. But the first time she had visited the clinic she had not been like that. It had taken two years of treatments and failed procedures for her skin to thicken so much. The first time she had come to the clinic and written her name in the register, she had noticed a lot of things. And looking at the age of the other women who were waiting to see the doctor, she had wondered if she was already too late. Apparently there were women as much as 8 to 10 years younger than her who were at the clinic to get fertility treatments. What had she been doing ten years ago? Well, ten years ago there were other things to worry about.

One morning, about ten years ago, Seema's cook had not shown up in the morning and the packet of milk that the milkman had plopped into the bag hung at her door had been unceremoniously dumped into the fridge by her flatmate, Anu.

"I'll take care of this in the evening," Anu had said to Seema as she rushed out of the flat, already late for the office.

Seema too had quickly grabbed a granola bar from a shelf in her kitchen and rushed out of her flat. But in the evening, when Seema had reached home from the office, she had received a message from Anu, 'Shantanu's meeting cancelled. See you Monday.'

Shantanu was Anu's boyfriend and things had started to escalate between them. There was talk of a possible engagement soon. With the flat all to herself for the weekend, Seema decided to call Abhi.

"Hey Babe!" his sexy voice answered her phone call.

"What plans for the weekend, Mr. Abhimanyu?"

"I'll leave the office in another 20 minutes. So, you tell me. Do we have plans?"

"Well... Anu is away for the weekend..."

"I'm leaving now."

"Pick up some beer on the way. I'll order pizza."

"I love you."

"I love you too. See you soon."

Abhi arrived soon enough and Seema opened the door to her flat.

"Offerings for the lovely lady!" he announced, holding a six pack of beer.

She smiled at him and pecked him on his lips as she noted how delicious he looked in his formal shirt and dark trousers. He was a couple of inches taller than her and there was something about his black close cropped hair and bronze clean shaven face that went so well with formal attire. He was even wearing a tie that day. Maybe there had been an important meeting. He slid his perfectly polished leather shoes off his feet and walked to the dining table to deposit the beer and his bag. Seema closed the door and walked into the kitchen.

"What are you doing?" he asked her as he followed her into the kitchen.

"Just boiling some milk," she said.

"Hmmm..." Abhi noted as he loosened his tie and started to unbutton his shirt.

"We have stuff we need to talk about," she said, eyeing him.

They hadn't seen each other in a week and looking at him unbuttoning his shirt like that was making her lose her self-control.

"You know I hate sitting around in formals once I'm back from the office," he said as he proceeded to tug his shirt out from his trousers.

"Go to the bedroom and change," she said.

"But I didn't get a change of clothes," said Abhi, peering into the *bhagona* of milk on the stove, "I came straight from the office."

"I have your old T-shirt and a few other things in my cupboard," she informed him.

"Wow! How did I not notice that some of my clothes were missing? And why have you been stealing my clothes?" he teased her as he walked to her and stood facing her with his hands on his hips, his eyes narrowed in accusation.

"I'm sure you knew about it! In fact I'm sure you sneaked them into my bag at the resort that weekend!" She protested vehemently, her eyes rounded in disbelief.

"And why would I do that?" He asked her with a smile.

"I thought it was a hint from you about, you know, wanting us to spend more time with each other or something," she said, averting her gaze from him, suddenly feeling an unexpected bout of shyness.

"You needed hints? I thought I was pretty clear when I told you that I would spend every minute of every day with you if I could!" he reminded her in disbelief.

"Well... One can't believe all the things one hears in the middle of or right after... you know..." she went on, her gaze shifting again to his face.

"You know? Is that what we're calling it now? So are we doing 'you know' tonight?"

"We'll see about that later. Just go to my room. Your stuff is on the middle shelf in my cupboard."

Abhi pecked her on her lips and was soon on his way to Seema's bedroom. The pizza had arrived shortly after that and soon Seema and Abhi sat on her couch in the living room and had a little chat.

"Why can't you just stay put here?" Seema finally asked him, "We can get married and move in together. Then we can workout together every day and eat dinner together every day and just be with each other."

"All that sounds really tempting," he responded as he picked up a slice of pizza from the cardboard box, "I want that life with you too. It's just that right now I feel like focusing on my career. This move to Bangalore is really going to give my career a boost."

"You could always shop around for other jobs in Mumbai," she suggested.

"Why don't you look for jobs in Bangalore?" he retorted, "I'm sure you'll find something."

"But I like my job here," she said, "I'm doing so well. I might even get promoted soon. I don't think that this is the right time for me to leave the company."

They talked about it at great lengths and decided that they would take their chances at being in a long distance relationship for a while.

About a year and a half after that, Seema was overjoyed when Abhi moved back to Mumbai. They got married and moved in together. It was a glorious time in their life. Getting to spend so much time with each other seemed like such a blessing. They simply couldn't keep their hands off of each other.

"Hey Abhi," Seema asked one night as she lay on the bed with her head on Abhi's chest, "do you want to have a baby?"

"It's been only a year since we got married," he said as he ran his fingers through her hair, "What's the rush?"

A few months after that Seema had some disagreements with her new boss at the office. He was a bit of an asshole. Not as mature as her previous boss who had left the company for a more lucrative job. Seema decided to switch jobs. She applied for many jobs in Mumbai but finally ended up saying yes to a job in Delhi.

"I'm sure we'll be fine," Abhi assured her, "We have done this long distance thing before. I know how much your career means to you."

And this time she was the one who left Abhi behind in Mumbai.

After spending a respectable amount of time at the job in Delhi, Seema started to search for jobs in Mumbai. After all, they had invested a lot of money into buying a property in Mumbai and it made sense to settle down there. By the time she moved back to Mumbai and settled down in her job there, Seema had started to notice a couple of white strands in her hair. She noticed that it was beginning to get more difficult to shed weight once she gained it. And one day she realised that she really wanted to have a baby. Abhi agreed to it rather readily. But when they didn't get pregnant even after trying for one year, Seema insisted that they visit a doctor.

"It's more common than you would imagine," the doctor said, "many women end up with blocked fallopian tubes. You could try some procedures to unblock them. But I would suggest IVF, given your husband's low sperm count and your low ovarian reserve. For your kind of prognosis, IVF has a good success rate."

Abhi had been very unaccepting of the whole situation.

"We have talked about this before Seema," he reminded her, "Remember when Pinky Didi went through her whole ordeal? We had decided that we would never get into anything like this. We had decided that we would be happy to have a baby if you got pregnant but we had decided we would never go to those limits."

"I know," Seema responded, "I know what I said back then. But you heard what the doctor said. My case has high chances of success."

It had taken almost a year to get Abhi on board and by the time Seema wrote her name onto the register at the fertility clinic for the first time, she was well into her thirties. But most of her friends had given birth in their thirties. Granted they had been in their early thirties, but so what? Seema wasn't that old. The doctor believed that it could have been an unrelated illness that could have affected her fallopian tubes but other than that there did not seem to be anything to worry about. Seema was optimistic.

"I'll just try this once," she had promised Abhi, "just one round of IVF. And if it doesn't work then we can think about adoption."

"I'm not so sure about adoption," Abhi had responded, "wouldn't it be nicer to have a baby that looked like us?"

"Yes," Seema said, "But I really want us to be parents. I want to be a mother, Abhi. I want a baby that we can take care of. I feel like I would be willing to adopt if it really came to that."

"Let's hope this works out and then we won't have to have that conversation," Abhi said.

But the thing is, it hadn't worked. They had been hopeful because Seema responded to the hormones and they were able to fertilise enough embryos for three transfers. But after every transfer, the pregnancy tests had turned out to be negative. After the third negative pregnancy test Abhi had confided in Seema, "To tell you the truth, Babe, I never really wanted to have kids in the first place. Let's just forget about all this. Let's just go back to living life like we did before."

But Seema had been adamant.

"I want to give it another shot," She had responded, "God knows we have enough money for 10 IVFs and even surrogacy if we really want to go for it!"

"I have a lot of work to do right now. I have an important meeting tomorrow morning," Abhi had said and vanished into his study room.

This round of IVF had been a lot more lonely for Seema than the last one. Abhi was fed up with her by now. Getting over another negative pregnancy test after the first transfer had all but broken Seema. She had been hanging by a mere thread when the second transfer resulted in a positive pregnancy test.

"Let's not get too excited before we confirm by sonography," the doctor had warned her, "your numbers are acceptable but not that high."

So, Seema really needed to know that day. She really needed to know what the sonography results were. Even though the result would not change even if she postponed her appointment by a day like Abhi had suggested, she knew that she had to know as soon as she could. Even if it meant going to the clinic on her own.

The doctor finally arrived and Seema entered her office hesitantly. The doctor had her usual no-nonsense expression on her face that didn't really give away anything.

"I have the results, Seema," the doctor said, "and it doesn't look good."

Seema was too numb to feel anything by then. She just wanted to know. Whatever happened. Either way. She just needed to know.

"What does that mean?" she asked the doctor.

"The pregnancy is not progressing the way we had hoped," the doctor told her, "It got implanted but the embryo isn't growing. I'm so sorry, Seema. There is no point continuing your support hormones any longer. You can stop taking the medication."

"Okay," said Seema.

"It's too early in the pregnancy to need any procedure," the doctor explained, "I'll give you some pills and that'll take care of it. The cramps might be painful."

Seema took her prescription and walked out of the doctor's office. She walked straight to the pharmacy, bought the pill, kept it in her purse, and drove back home.

It had been a long day at the office and Abhi was exhausted. He fished the keys out of his pocket and opened the door to his flat. He turned on the light of the small gallery at the entrance and sat down on the brown wooden bench. After taking off his shoes he walked into the living area that was illuminated by a lone lamp in the corner. With a spot of music the ambience could have been romantic but the whole setting just seemed gloomy to Abhi. In fact most settings seemed gloomy to him these days. There was a time when he used to walk into a home filled with music but these days there was silence. Utter, soul crushing silence. He started to walk across the room to make his way to the bedroom. He couldn't wait to get out of his formal clothes. But he stopped as soon as he saw Seema. He hadn't seen her smile in a long time but the way she was sitting on the couch and just staring at the blank television in front of her kind of scared him. He turned around and deposited his bag on the dining table. He walked over to the couch and sat next to Seema.

"Did you have anything to eat?" he asked her.

She didn't say anything and continued to stare listlessly at the television.

"What did the doctor say?" he asked her softly.

Her face transformed as she glanced at him with angry eyes.

"How does it matter to you? You don't even want kids," she snapped back at him.

"What did the doctor say, Seema?" asked Abhi, a bit sternly this time.

"You should be happy. It didn't work," she snapped at him again.

"I'm sorry, Babe," he said to her softly, "I know this meant a lot to you."

"You have no idea," she said, "you have no idea what it meant to me."

"That's why I didn't want you to go today," said Abhi, trying his best to control the anger that welled up inside him at the tone in which she was talking to him, "We both knew that there was a chance that this could happen."

"So your way of dealing with it was to postpone it for another day?" Seema accused him, "One extra day of taking that fucking medication that screws my body and screws my mind over!"

"I just wanted to be able to wish you a happy anniversary at midnight," Abhi confided in her, "Of course now I sound like an asshole for bringing that up... Now that..."

"Oh..." Seema said softly, the anger in her eyes giving way to sadness, "I didn't realise... I... I forgot..."

"I miss my wife," said Abhi, his anger subsiding as he noticed a change in Seema's tone, "I miss you Seema. The Seema from before all this... this obsession of having a baby."

"Let's just forget all this," Seema relented, looking at her hands that lay in her lap, "Let's go somewhere. Let's go somewhere far away from here."

"Where do you want to go?" Abhi asked her.

"I don't know," she said, "Maybe we can go to Singapore. I can take a couple of days off next month. I know you've been wanting to visit Atul and Teena."

"Are you sure you're going to be okay?" said Abhi, taking her hand into his, "They had another baby recently."

"I..." Seema stuttered, her throat choked with emotion, "I know... I know what happened on the flight to Delhi... when the lady and her baby were sitting next to me... but I can't avoid babies all my life... I have to... I have to learn to be fine with all this. I have to learn to not fall apart and burst into tears in the presence of a baby..."

"Let's go to Sri Lanka instead," suggested Abhi, "Just the two of us."

Seema looked at him and said, "I'll book the resort."

He smiled at her and said, "I'll book the flight."

"I have to stop the medication from today," she told him, "and all the restrictions that the doctor told us about don't apply from today."

"How about beer, pizza and Passengers?" he asked her.

"For Jennifer Lawrence, I'm sure," she teased him.

"Well, I thought you said that Chris Pratt really cleaned up nice for this one," he said, giving her a knowing smile.

"Yeah, he looked pretty hot in Passengers," she said, nodding her head thoughtfully, "Beer, pizza, Passengers... sounds good."

After more than a year Seema agreed to touch alcohol. After more than a year, Abhi and Seema watched a movie together, even if it wasn't in the theatre. After more than a year, Seema lay down on the couch with her head in Abhi's lap. By the time the movie was over, she was fast asleep. Abhi slid her head onto a pillow and got up from the couch. He threw away the empty pizza box and empty cans of beer.

He covered Seema's frail body with a light blanket and sat down on the floor next to the couch. He took her left hand into his hands and looked at the simple gold band that she wore on her ring finger. He kissed the back of her hand and said, "Why am I not enough for you, Babe? Why do you need another person in your life? If you need someone to take care of, why can't you just take care of me? And I promise I'll take care of you too."

ᑭᑭᑭ

rdinarily, trying to get pregnant can be quite a bit of fun for a couple. But the way Seema needed to get pregnant meant that they had to abstain for long periods of time.

"No vigorous physical activity," the doctor had insisted on multiple occasions.

And even if there were short periods of time when physical activities were technically allowed, Abhi and Seema had simply not been on the same page. She had just been too grouchy the past year or so for Abhi to even approach her. But in the last month or so, since they had put a stop to the fertility treatments after the disappointing sonogram, Seema had begun to improve. She had started to look much better than she had in the previous year. Abhi had finally managed to convince her to get a haircut. When she got back from the salon, she almost smiled. It made Abhi's heart skip a beat. The straight shoulder length hair framed her face just right. Her lips glistened. Her eyes didn't quite twinkle but she was getting there. His wife, who he had missed so dearly for so long, seemed to be on her way back. She plopped her bag on the dining table and walked up to him. Sitting next to him on the couch, she leaned towards him and asked him, "What plans for the weekend, Mr. Abhimanyu?"

And he knew that this was his cue.

That night Seema unbuttoned Abhi's shirt after a long time. That night Abhi slid her skirt off after a long time. And after a long time, Abhi and Seema expressed their love for each other in the most intimate way.

# 4

Sri Lanka was beautiful. The food was amazing and the beaches were clean. Seema felt the sand beneath her feet and the cool breeze on her face. She looked at the heavenly ball of fire beginning to dip into the calm ocean. The last rays of the sun dancing on the waves, the sounds of the waves lashing at the beach, the fragrance of the barbecue simmering a few metres away from her. Everything seemed to be perfect. But she had an empty feeling inside of her. As if a part of her was missing. Abhi soon walked up to her and took her hand into his. When she turned to look at him, she also saw the glimmer of a flame behind him. She tilted her head and noticed a middle aged man lighting a lantern with a torch. There was an endless row of lanterns hanging on wooden poles that lined the beach. The man moved from one lantern to the next, illuminating them with the flame at the tip of the torch he was carrying. Seema moved her attention back to the sun. It was almost gone. It had vanished behind the waves, leaving a magnificent sky in its wake. A sky coloured in hues of orange, pink and blue. A sky adorned with tufts of grey and white. A sky that would soon be engulfed in darkness.

Seema and Abhi began walking along the beach, taking in the beauty around them. Seema saw his calm features and almost abandoned her resolve. But then she told herself that she had to do it. She had thought about this for the past couple of months and she had made up her mind that she needed to share this with Abhi. She would never be okay if she didn't share it with him. He deserved to know. And she needed to tell him.

"You want to go to the bar?" Abhi asked her.

"Let's go back to the room," she suggested.

As they made their way back to the beachside resort, Seema turned back to look at the beach again. It looked so different than it had barely minutes ago. The sky was dark. But against this dark backdrop, the row of lanterns that were now lit up looked magical. Nature could be really beautiful. And so could human inventions.

Seema and Abhi walked on a narrow path that led them to the main building of the resort. They took the elevator to their floor and made their way to their room. Their room in the resort was luxurious. The floor length curtains, the wall mounted TV, the king size bed, a sitting area with a cream coloured couch. It was well laid out and did not seem cluttered. Every time Seema walked into the room she noticed how it had a lot of space for a child to play. Across the sitting area was a balcony with a view of the swimming pool. Abhi walked out to the balcony and stood there looking down at the pool. He had a faint smile on his lips. Seema walked over and stood beside him. She saw that a young family was trying to get their toddler out of the pool. The kid seemed to not want to follow his mother's instructions.

"Abhi," said Seema, "I need to talk to you about something."

He looked at her and she continued, "When we started trying to have a baby, I was sure that I would get pregnant in no time. When I didn't, the whole situation came out of nowhere. It just shook me."

"You know what the doctors said," said Abhi, "no matter how healthy you are, you never know about your fertility until you actually get pregnant."

"The thing is," Seema finally told him, "I was pregnant... I was pregnant a long time ago and so I was sure that I would be able to get pregnant very easily."

Abhi's forehead became furrowed. "What are you talking about?" he asked her.

"You remember that time when you got that job in Bangalore," said Seema, "we weren't even married back then. I... I was pregnant."

Abhi's face became ashen as he stood there, staring at her in disbelief.

"How could you have been pregnant?" he asked her.

"You know how Abhi. You know how people usually get pregnant."

"But we... we were careful..."

"It happens... there is always a small chance of getting pregnant."

"But why didn't you tell me?"

"By the time I found out you were already in Bangalore."

"I was in Bangalore but we used to talk every single day. How could you keep this from me?"

"I... I thought about telling you..."

"What did you do, Seema? What did you do to our baby?"

The horror and the pain that Seema saw in Abhi's eyes that day was something she would never forget.

"I thought you never wanted kids," she said softly, looking into Abhi's eyes, "whatever happened... how does it matter to you?"

"You have got to be kidding me Seema!" he yelled at her, "How could you get rid of my baby without even talking to me about it? How could you do this to me?"

Seema looked around and people from the pool were beginning to look up to their balcony.

"Let's talk inside," she pleaded.

"I can't be in the same room as you right now," he declared, "I need some air."

He walked into the room and kept walking towards the door.

"Wait! Abhi! It's not what you think!" she called out as she followed him.

He stopped in his tracks but didn't turn around to look at her.

"I..." she said, "You know... by the time I realised that I was pregnant, it had been a few months. You know how my period can be irregular sometimes. I just didn't notice for some time. But then, when I did, I decided that I should be sure about it before I talked to you about it. When the blood test came out positive, the doctor said that I should wait till the sonography report to tell anyone."

Abhi turned around and looked at her.

"I'm sure the father of the baby is not just anyone," he said.

"I..." stammered Seema and lowered her gaze to the floor, "and... even back then... it didn't stick... the pregnancy didn't stick... even back then I lost our baby... there was... there should have been a heartbeat but they couldn't find one... and... and... I..."

As tears streamed down Seema's cheek and her heart broke into pieces yet again, she felt the warmth of Abhi's body as he enveloped her into a warm hug.

"Abhi..." Seema continued in her quavering voice, " Abhi... I sometimes feel like I'm being punished... I feel like I'm being punished for what I did..."

"You didn't do anything, Babe," he whispered as his eyes welled up with tears.

"I..." she continued, "I can't believe that I was relieved... I was relieved and almost happy... The first time we lost our baby I was happy... because it meant that we didn't have to take a call... that we didn't have to change our plans... Abhi... I can't believe... I can't believe..."

"It wasn't your fault, Babe," Abhi tried to reassure her, "That was a different time... It's not your fault..."

"Why am I not enough, Abhi?" she wailed, "Why was my body not able to take care of our babies?"

"It's not your fault. None of this is anybody's fault."

A lot of tears were shed in the hotel room that night as Abhi and Seema cried for the loss that they had never mourned before.

ᐅᐅᐅ

The next morning was unusual. Abhi was a sunset person but he was on the beach to watch the sunrise with Seema.

"It has always annoyed me how you love kids," Seema confided in him, "You love other peoples' kids but you always say that you don't want us to have kids of our own."

"Remember when we first started trying to get pregnant?" Abhi asked her, "Do you ever remember me saying then that I didn't want kids?"

"I don't know," said Seema, "we didn't talk about it that much back then I guess."

"I was actually looking forward to it at that time," he said, "to see you with a huge belly and a glowing face. To have a baby who would look like you. But at some point... I know you tried to hide it from me but I noticed how much you cried every time you had your period. And you have never been a baby person. You never took the babies of any of your friends in your arms. So I thought that you were stressing out about having a baby for my sake. I would have been happy if we had a baby but I don't want a baby if having a baby is going to… if it's going to mess us up. For me, you and I are enough."

Seema took Abhi's hand into hers and rested her head on his shoulder.

"I know I'm not a baby person but having a baby is not just about having a baby," said Seema, "the baby grows up and becomes a toddler and then a teenager and then an adult. Being a parent is so much more than taking care of a baby or playing with a toddler. I want to experience that. I don't know why. I just really really want that for us. I want us to have a family."

"We are a family Babe," said Abhi, "You and I. We are a family."

"I know… I love you… but… are you willing to try one last time?" she asked him, "We have one last batch of embryos. We can try one last transfer for IVF. I promise I'll listen to you. I'll try my best not to become obsessive about it."

"After your last transfer, when you were lying down in that room," said Abhi, "I had a chat with the doctor. She said that if the treatments don't work we can try surrogacy. And if we are not willing to do that then she can sign some papers that will make it easier for us to adopt."

"Let's go to the doctor and discuss our options with her again," said Seema.

# 5

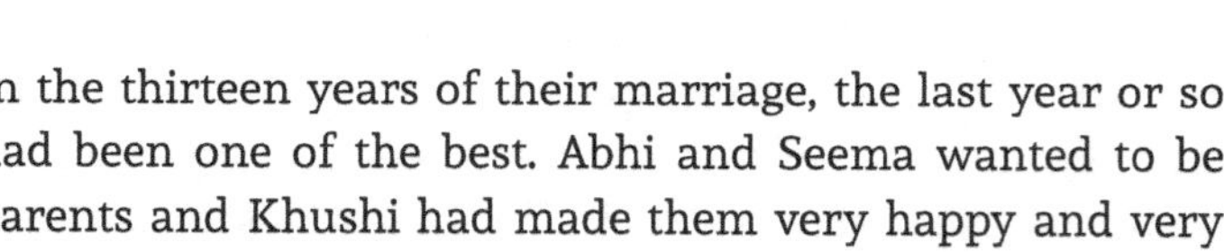

In the thirteen years of their marriage, the last year or so had been one of the best. Abhi and Seema wanted to be parents and Khushi had made them very happy and very proud parents. Of course there had been mood swings and tantrums and visits to the doctor along the way but all in all, they were a happy family.

"One more bedtime story Papa," Khushi begged and there was no way Abhi could ever say no to her pouting face.

"Fine," he relented, "but you'll have to listen to it lying down. No jumping around for this one."

Then he tucked Khushi into her white toddler bed, covering her with her favourite yellow blanket.

"Which one is it going to be?" he asked her.

"Goldilocks!" she squealed excitedly.

"Okay," said Abhi and pulled out a book from the bookshelf next to the bed. Then he pulled a little red chair next to the bed and cleared his throat.

"Why aren't you asleep yet?" Seema interjected, peeping into the room, "baby, if you don't go to sleep on time then you won't be able to get up in the morning. You don't want to be late to go to the zoo, right?"

"I'll sleep soon Mummy," replied Khushi.

"It's the last story," Abhi explained.

"Okay," said Seema.

She pulled another little red chair and sat next to Abhi as he animatedly read out the story from the book. By the time the story ended, little Khushi was half-asleep. Seema switched off the light and stood behind Abhi who was unable to take his eyes off the glowing face of his daughter.

"Let's leave the table-lamp on," Seema whispered into his ear, "last time she freaked out when she woke up in the middle of the night because it was too dark."

"Hmmm..." responded Abhi, still gazing at his daughter.

Seema kept her hands on Abhi's shoulders and whispered into his ear, "What plans for the weekend, Mr. Abhimanyu?"

Abhi finally tore his eyes away from his daughter and smiled at his wife.

They were enough.

# Author's Request To The Readers

If you like what I write, please post reviews on Amazon and Goodreads. I would really like to know your views about my book.

# About The Author

An IITian, an alumnus of The Ohio State University, a professionally trained scientist currently teaching at a University in Central India, Venuka Goyal has lived in the world of academics all her life. While her profession has involved reading scientific literature, she also read a lot of fiction while growing up. From Enid Blyton to the Bronte sisters, from Harry Potter to Nancy Drew, she loved novels as much as she loved her science textbooks in school. In her 15 year long career in science, Venuka published many scientific articles in international journals of repute. Emails addressed to 'Dear Author' have been a regular in her inbox for many years. During a lockdown Venuka started writing fiction to escape from the tough realities of a life that was turning out very different from what she had imagined and she accidentally ended up writing a novel. Her first novel 'You're stuck with me for life!' was published in August 2021 and was among the top hot releases in Kindle Store India. Since then there has been no looking back. Venuka writes contemporary fiction based on her experiences and focuses on the nature of relationships and marriage in modern India.

You can find Venuka on Instagram @venuka.goyal and Facebook @venuka.goyal.author